TERRY
PRATCHETT'S
DISCWORLD
COLOURING
BOOK

GOLLANCZ LONDON

Copyright © Terry and Lyn Pratchett
1986, 1988, 1989, 1990, 1991, 1993, 1994, 1995, 1996, 1999, 2000, 2001, 2003, 2016
Discworld® is a trademark registered by Terry Pratchett
Artwork copyright © Paul Kidby 2016
All rights reserved

The right of Terry Pratchett to be identified as the author of this work and the
right of Paul Kidby to be identified as the illustrator of this work has been asserted
by them in accordance with the Copyright, Designs and Patents Act 1988.

Quotations from *Interesting Times, Men At Arms, Maskerade, Thief of Time,
The Truth* and *Nanny Ogg's Cookbook* reproduced by kind permission of
Transworld Publishers. Quotations from *The Wee Free Men* reproduced by kind
permission of Penguin Random House UK Children's Books.

This edition first published in Great Britain in 2016 by Gollancz, an imprint of the
Orion Publishing Group
Carmelite House
50 Victoria Embankment
London EC4Y 0DZ
An Hachette UK Company

1 3 5 7 9 10 8 6 4 2

A CIP catalogue record for this book is available from the British Library

ISBN 978 1 473 21747 8

Printed in Italy

The Orion Publishing Group's policy is to use papers that are natural, renewable
and recyclable products and made from wood grown in sustainable forests.
The logging and manufacturing processes are expected to conform to the
environmental regulations of the country of origin.

www.discworld.com
www.terrypratchett.co.uk
www.paulkidby.com
www.orionbooks.co.uk
www.gollancz.co.uk
www.kismetphotography.co.uk

A Note from the Artist

For over twenty years I have had the pleasure of not only reading (and re-reading) Terry's Discworld novels but also of illustrating them. Designing his myriad characters with pencils and paint has challenged and amused me beyond measure. His writing conjures clear imagery in my mind's eye, triggering an imaginative pursuit to capture his humour and richly textured stories with my art.

Terry and I shared interests in nature, folklore, science and history; this common ground, (coupled with a love of Monty Python and the bizarre), brought our two crafts together with a collision of positive creative energy. It was an honour and a privilege to work with him.

In this book is a collection of some of my favourite characters, all carefully re-drafted as line art: witches, wizards, dragons and feegles await you. Have fun with your pens and pencils and I hope a little splash of Octarine, the colour of magic, glows from your finished pages.

My thanks to my wife, Vanessa, who worked alongside me on this project and to Harry Hall at Kismet Photography and Print whose mysterious digital skills enabled us to put the book together just as we envisioned. I wouldn't have managed without you both.

Paul Kidby

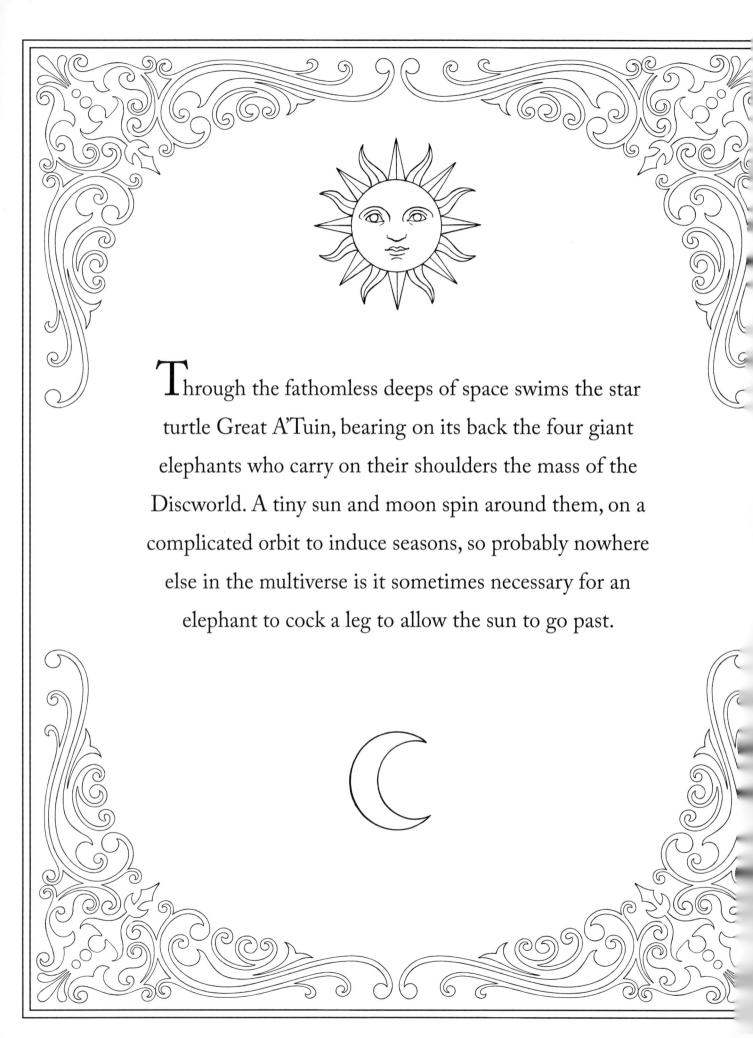

Through the fathomless deeps of space swims the star turtle Great A'Tuin, bearing on its back the four giant elephants who carry on their shoulders the mass of the Discworld. A tiny sun and moon spin around them, on a complicated orbit to induce seasons, so probably nowhere else in the multiverse is it sometimes necessary for an elephant to cock a leg to allow the sun to go past.

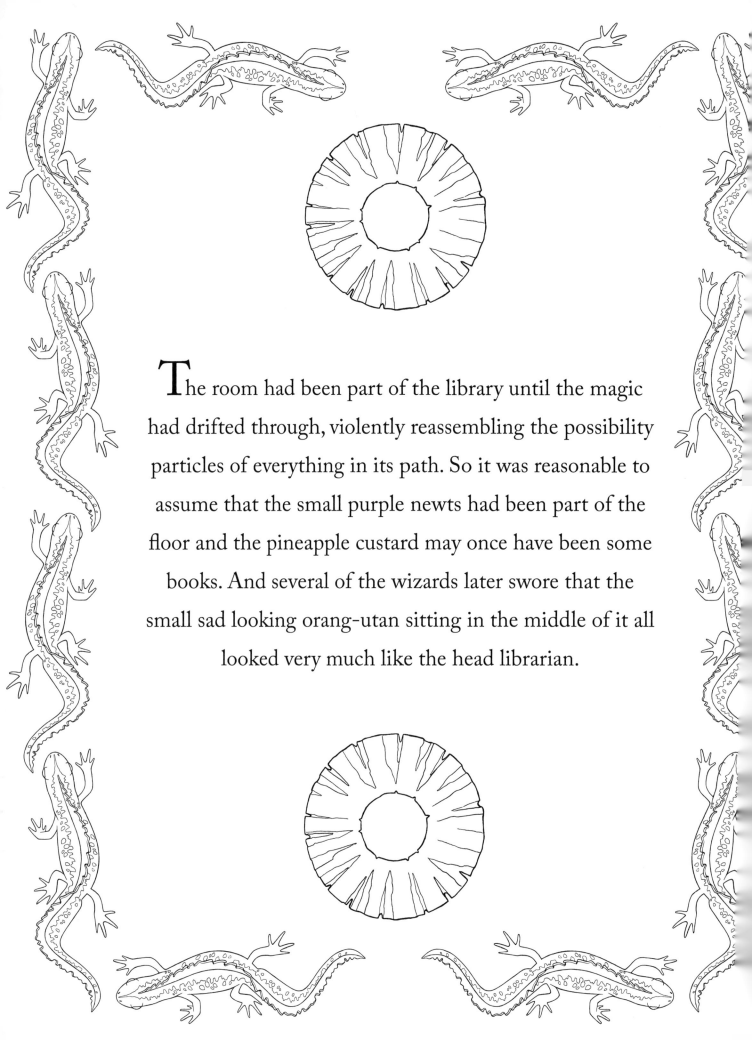

The room had been part of the library until the magic had drifted through, violently reassembling the possibility particles of everything in its path. So it was reasonable to assume that the small purple newts had been part of the floor and the pineapple custard may once have been some books. And several of the wizards later swore that the small sad looking orang-utan sitting in the middle of it all looked very much like the head librarian.

WHAT CAN
THE HARVEST
HOPE FOR,
IF NOT THE CARE
OF THE
REAPER MAN?

No other item in the entire
chronicle of travel accessories has
quite such a history of mystery and
grievous bodily harm.

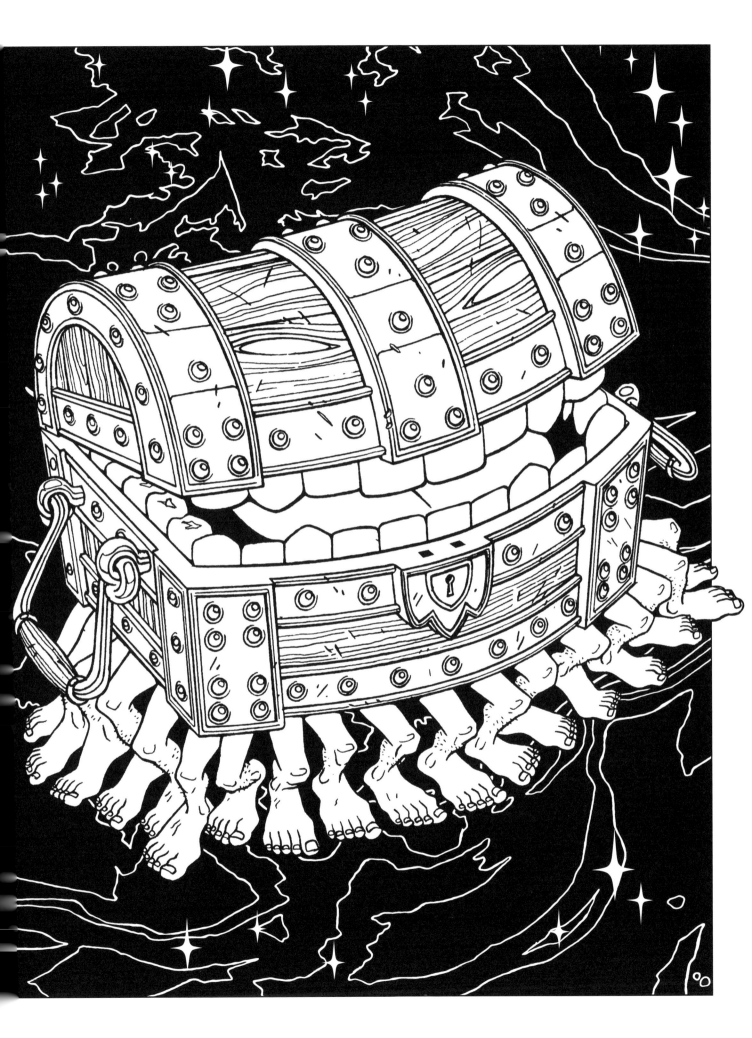

'What's the plan, Rob?'
said one of them.
'OK lads, this is what we'll do.
As soon as we see something,
we'll attack it. Right?'
The best plans are the simplest ones…

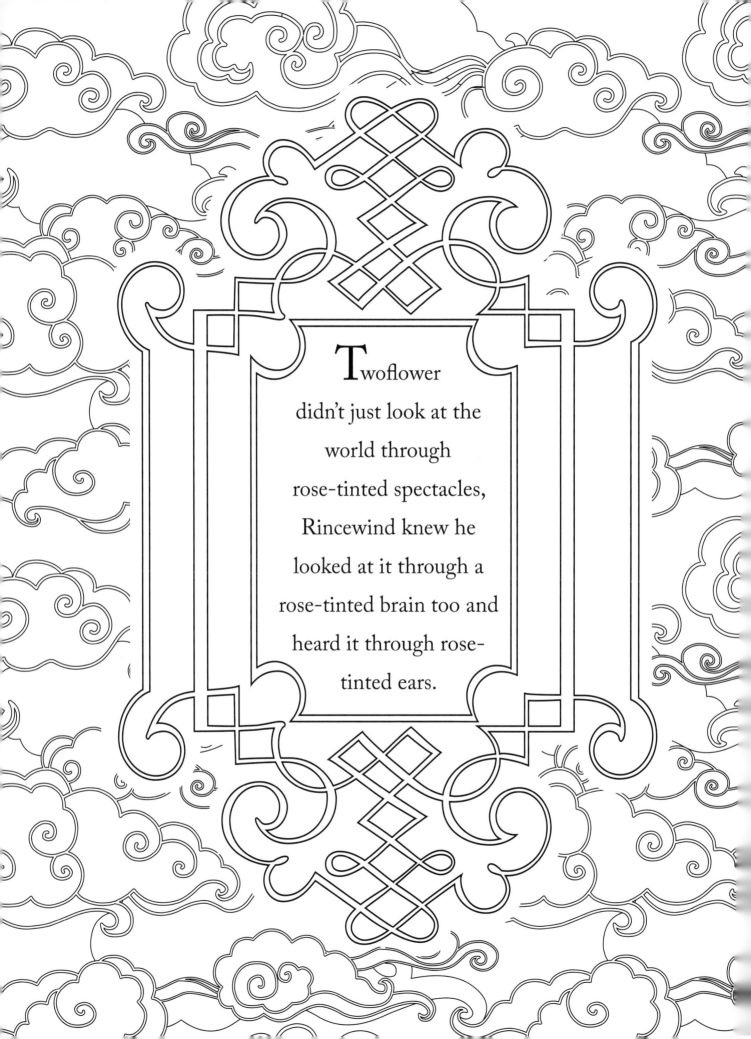

Twoflower didn't just look at the world through rose-tinted spectacles, Rincewind knew he looked at it through a rose-tinted brain too and heard it through rose-tinted ears.

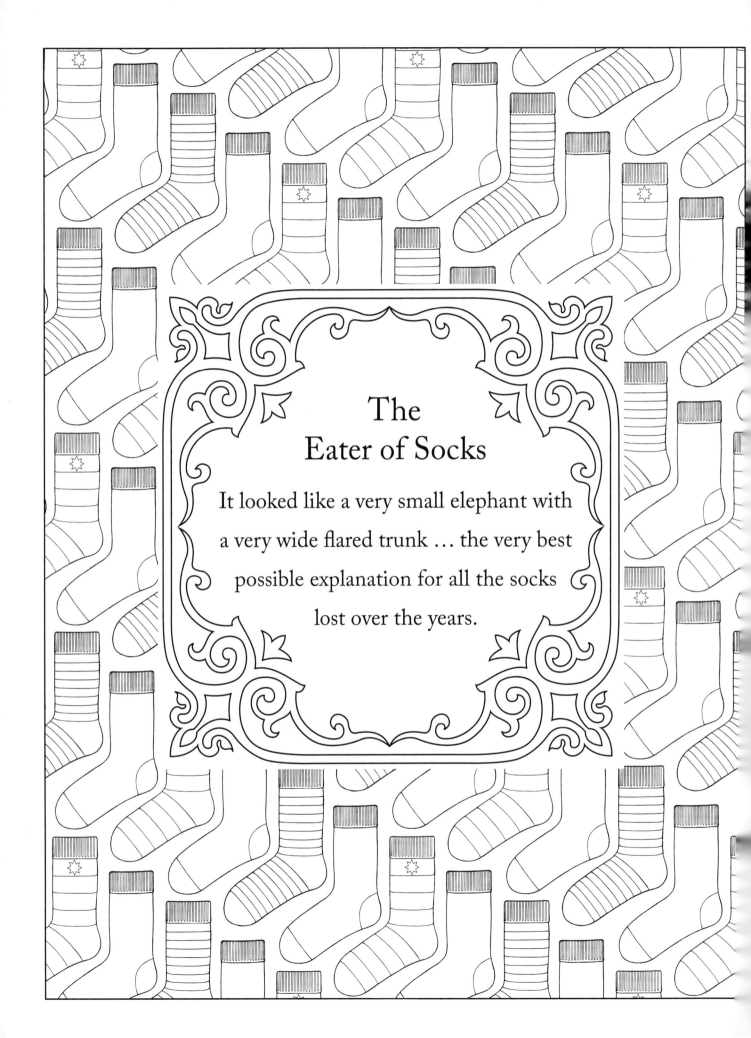

The
Eater of Socks

It looked like a very small elephant with a very wide flared trunk … the very best possible explanation for all the socks lost over the years.

Asmall elderly dragon had crawled out from under his chair and placed its jowly muzzle in Vimes's lap. It stared up at him soulfully with big brown eyes and gently dribbled something quite corrosive, by the feel of it, over his knees.

Susan was sensible. It was, she knew, a major character flaw. It did not make you popular, or cheerful, and – this seemed to her to be the most unfair bit – it didn't even make you right. But it did make you definite.

Modo straightened up, and paused to admire his rose-bed, which contained the finest display of pure black roses he'd ever managed to produce. A high magical environment could be useful, sometimes. Their scent hung on the evening air like an encouraging word.

The flower bed erupted.

Modo had a brief vision of flames and something arcing into the sky before his vision was blotted out by a rain of beads, feathers and soft black petals.
He shook his head and ambled off to fetch his shovel.

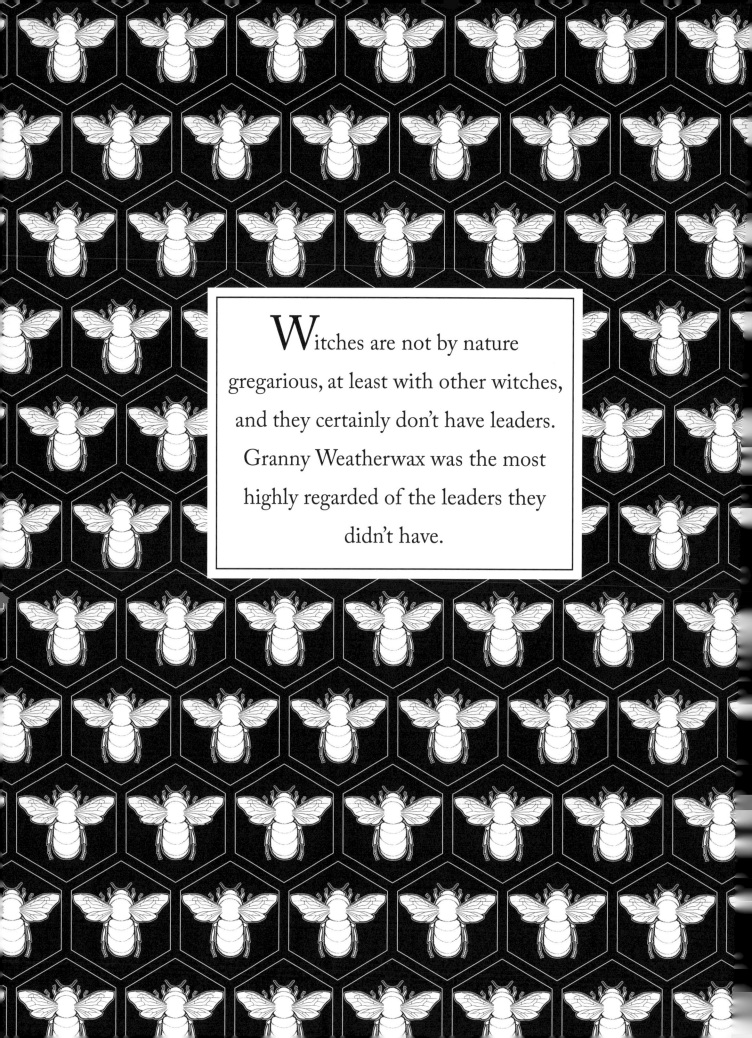

Witches are not by nature gregarious, at least with other witches, and they certainly don't have leaders. Granny Weatherwax was the most highly regarded of the leaders they didn't have.

'I know what you mean,' said Ponder. 'It's like pencils. I must have bought hundreds of pencils over the years, but how many have I ever actually worn down to the stub? Even I've caught myself thinking that something's creeping up and eating them.'

Hamish tumbled through the sky.
And then - something ballooned above
him and the fall became just a gentle
floating like thistledown.
He landed, and a pair of Tiffany's pants,
the ones with the rosebud pattern,
settled on top of him.

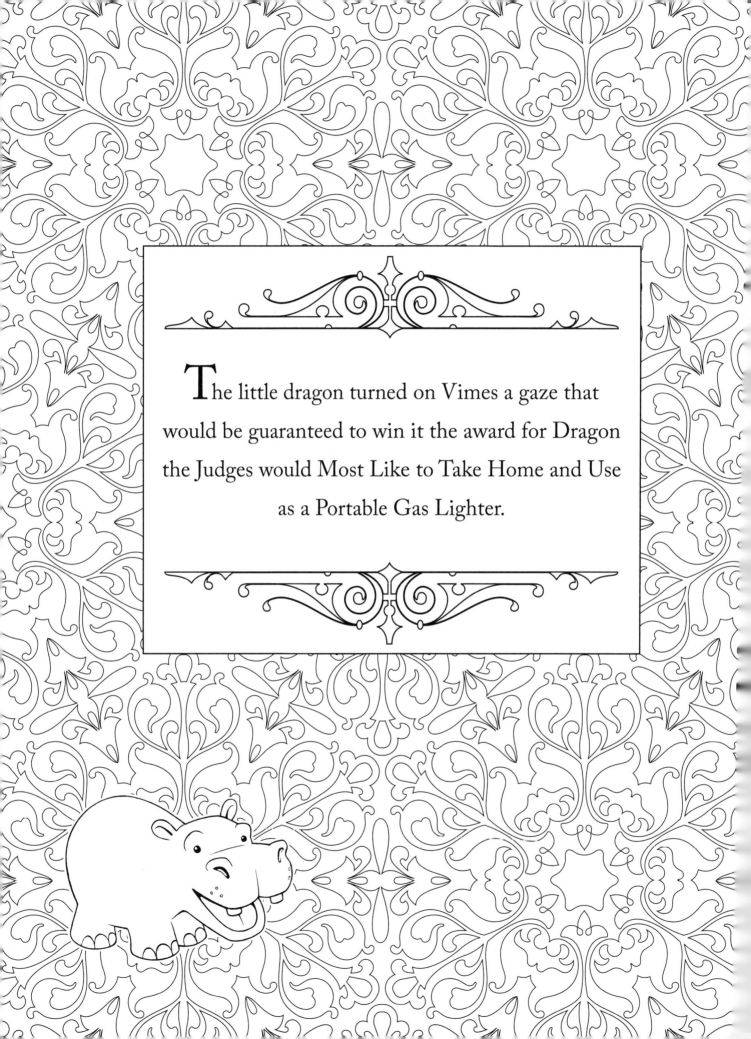

The little dragon turned on Vimes a gaze that would be guaranteed to win it the award for Dragon the Judges would Most Like to Take Home and Use as a Portable Gas Lighter.

'Luck is my middle name,' said
Rincewind, indistinctly. 'Mind you,
my first name is Bad.'

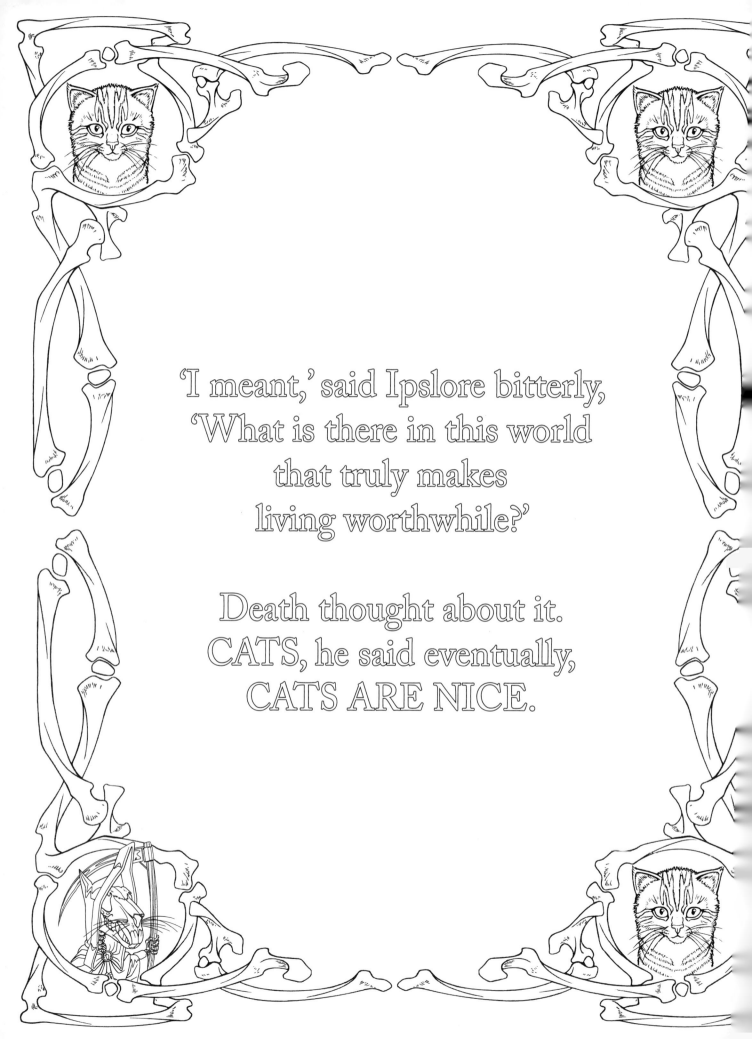

'I meant,' said Ipslore bitterly,
'What is there in this world
that truly makes
living worthwhile?'

Death thought about it.
CATS, he said eventually,
CATS ARE NICE.

For a moment the rank felt as though they had just returned from single-handedly conquering a distant province. They felt, in fact, tremendously bucked-up, which was how Lady Ramkin would almost certainly have put it and which was definitely several letters of the alphabet away from how they normally felt.

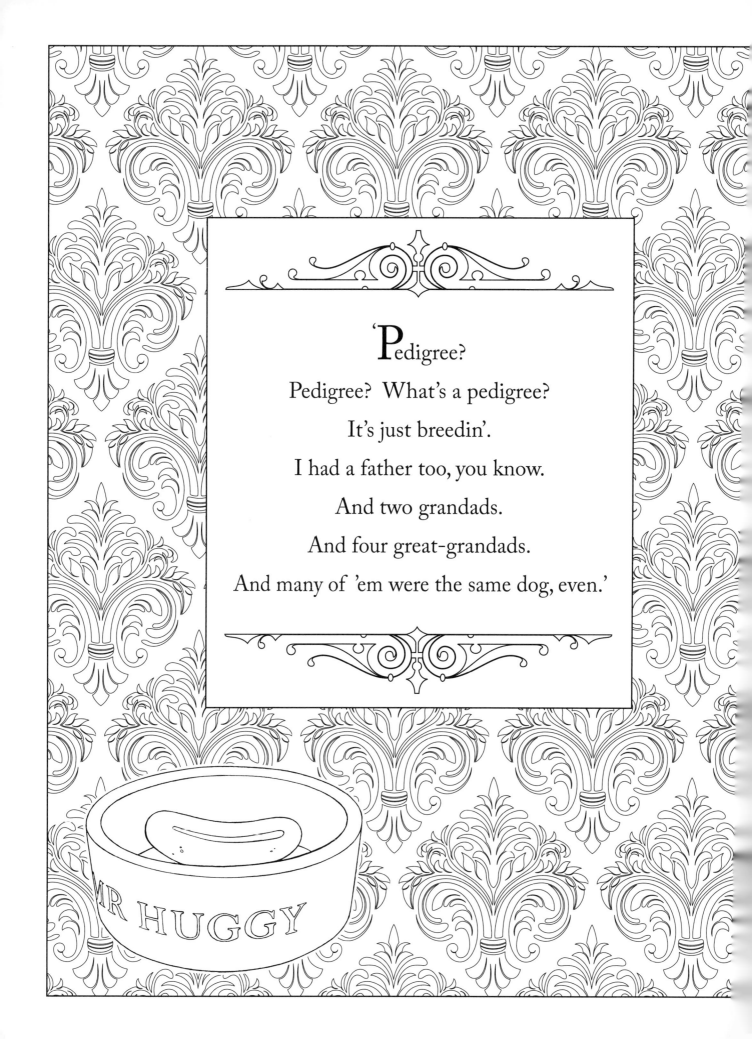

'Pedigree?

Pedigree? What's a pedigree?

It's just breedin'.

I had a father too, you know.

And two grandads.

And four great-grandads.

And many of 'em were the same dog, even.'

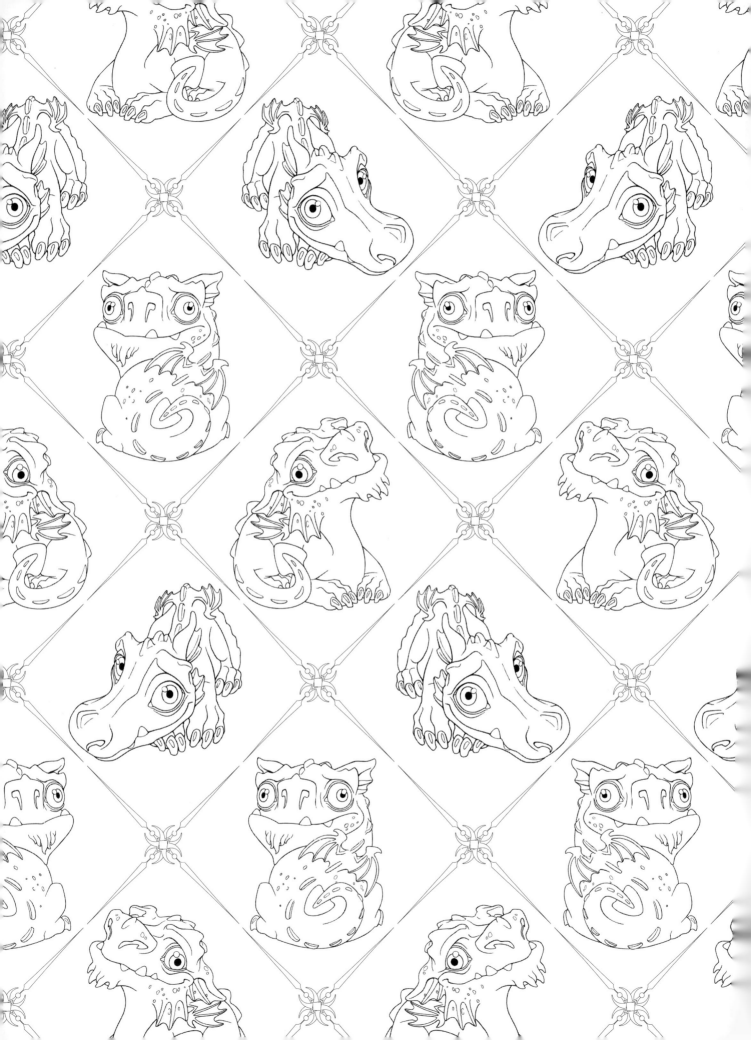

'Have you seen
Leonard da Quirm's
portrait of the Mona Ogg?
The teeth follow you around the room.
In fact some people said they followed
them out of the room
and all the way
down the street.'

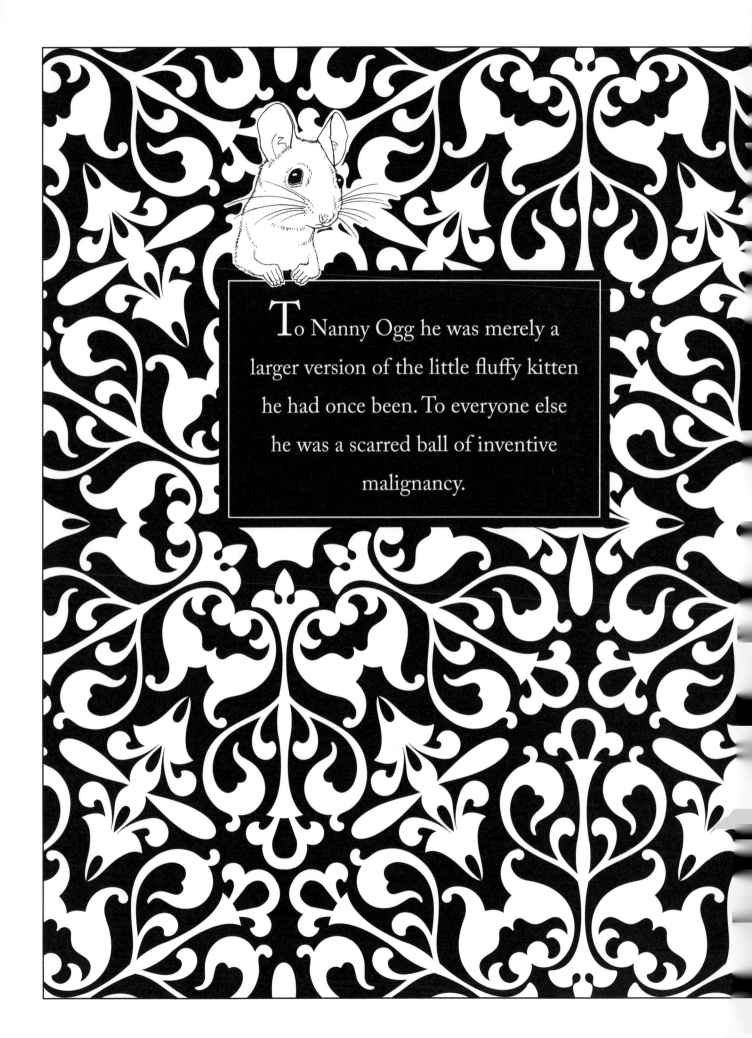

To Nanny Ogg he was merely a larger version of the little fluffy kitten he had once been. To everyone else he was a scarred ball of inventive malignancy.

'Every time you swear it comes alive,'
said the Senior Wrangler hurriedly,
'Ghastly little winged things
pop out of the air.'
'Bloody hellfire!'
said the Archchancellor.
Pop. Pop.

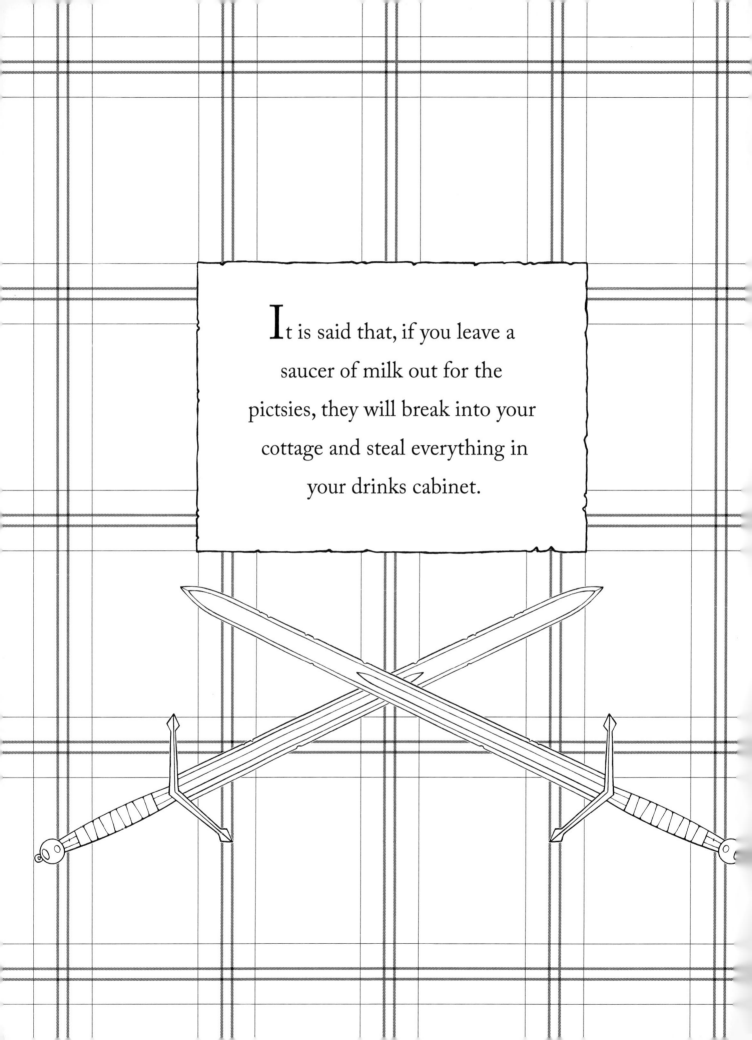

It is said that, if you leave a saucer of milk out for the pictsies, they will break into your cottage and steal everything in your drinks cabinet.

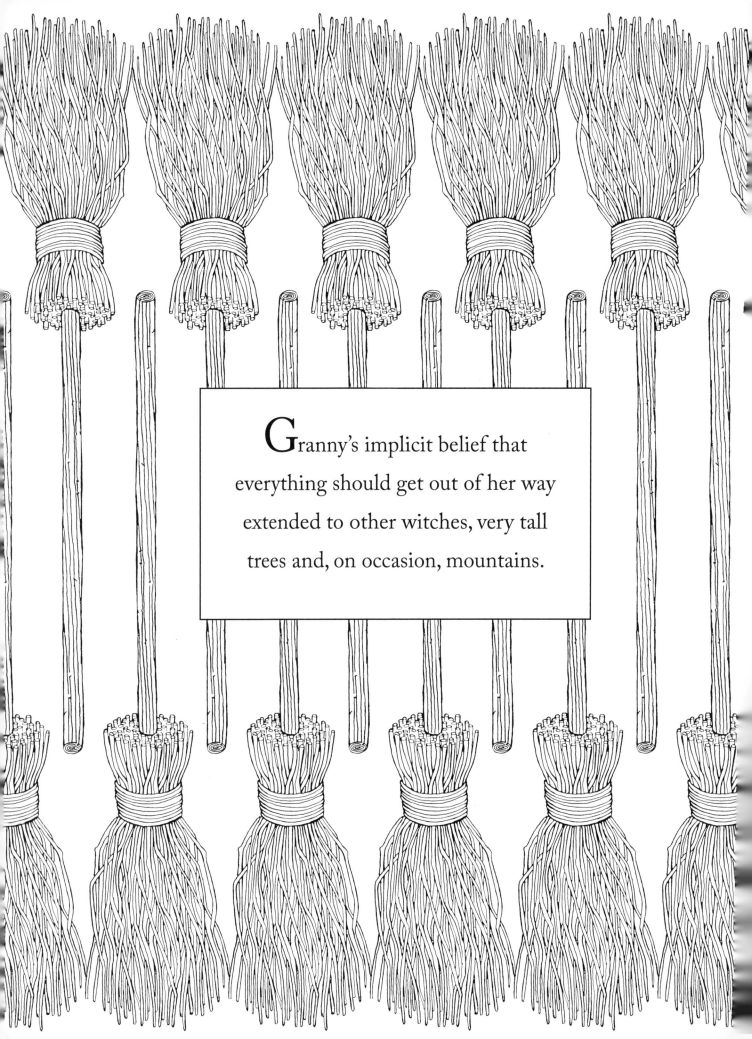

Granny's implicit belief that everything should get out of her way extended to other witches, very tall trees and, on occasion, mountains.

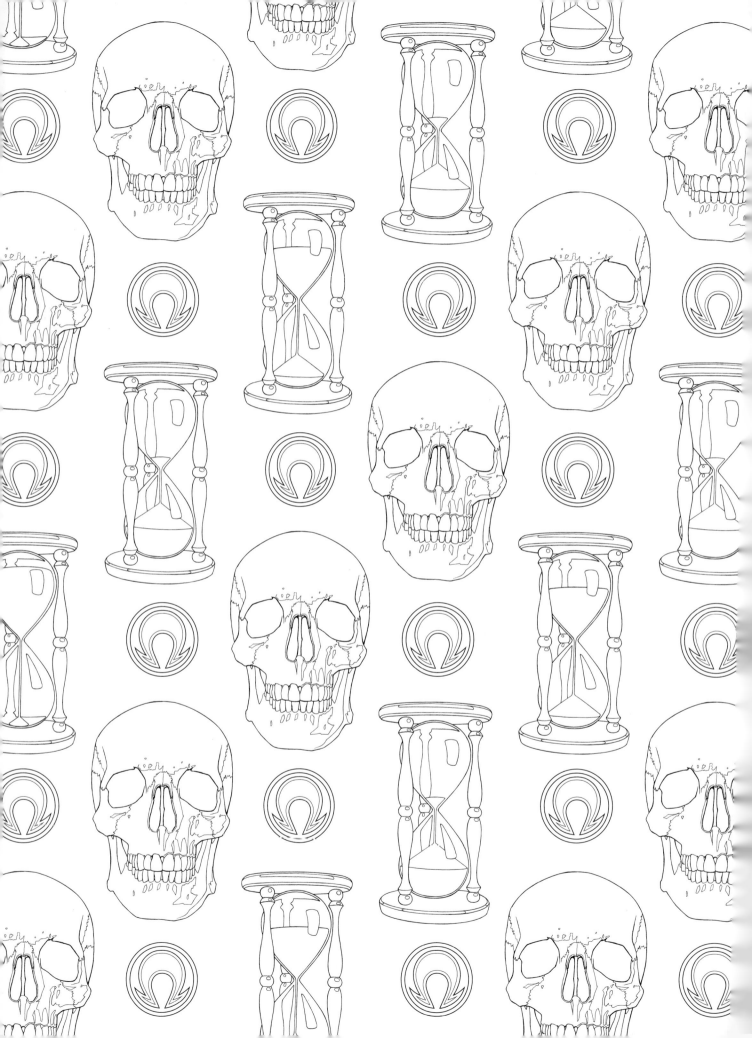

'My name is Otto Chriek.

I am a vizard in the darkroom.

Light is my canvas, shadows are my brush.

Be smiling, please!'

SQUEAK

It was said that Vetinari would tolerate absolutely
anything apart from anything that threatened the city.

And mime artists.

It was a strange aversion, but there you are. Anyone in
baggy trousers and a white face who tried to ply their
art anywhere within Ankh's crumbling walls would
very quickly find themselves in a scorpion pit, on one
wall of which was painted the advice:

LEARN THE WORDS.

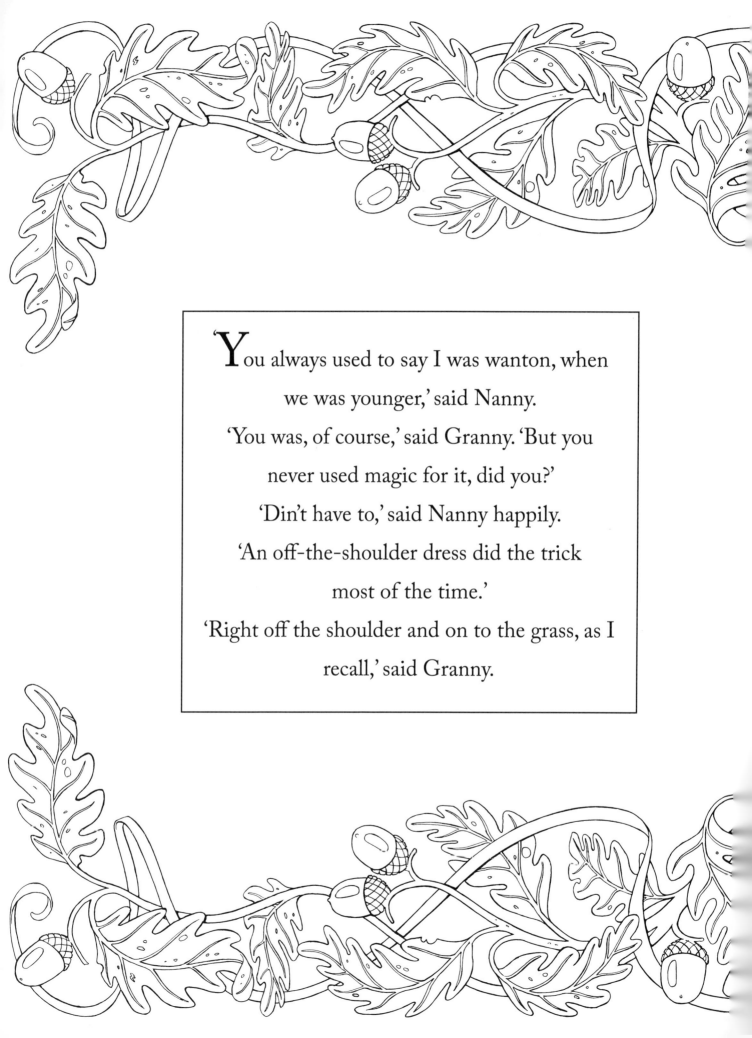

'You always used to say I was wanton, when
we was younger,' said Nanny.
'You was, of course,' said Granny. 'But you
never used magic for it, did you?'
'Din't have to,' said Nanny happily.
'An off-the-shoulder dress did the trick
most of the time.'
'Right off the shoulder and on to the grass, as I
recall,' said Granny.

He wore red:
a red suit with red lace,
a red cloak, red shoes with ruby
buckles, and a broad-brimmed
red hat with a huge red feather.
He even walked with a long
red stick, bedecked with
red ribbons.

The Quantum Weather Butterfly

(Papilio tempestae) is an undistinguished

yellow colour, although the mandelbrot

patterns on the wings are of considerable

interest. Its outstanding feature

is its ability to create weather.

The Colour of Magic *2011*

Death with Kitten II *2011*

Varieties of Swamp Dragon *2001*

Rincewind in the Dungeon Dimensions *1995*

The Finger of Cohen *2002*

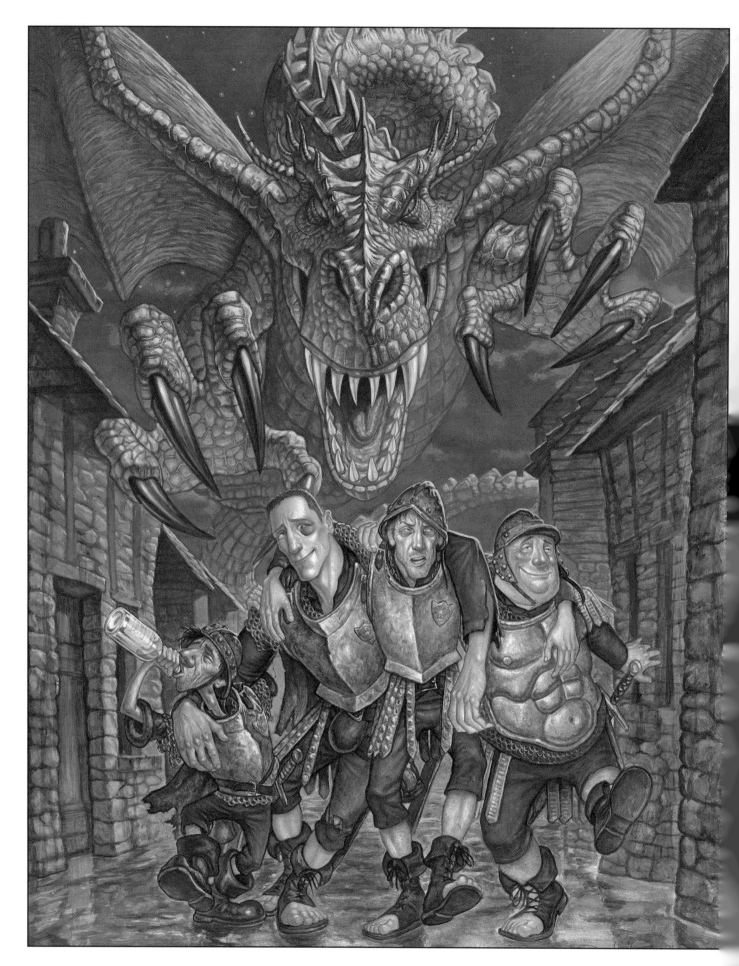

Feegle Horde *1998*

Wyrd Sisters *1995*